Leigh Hadley Irvine

Our Jim

The World's Champion

Leigh Hadley Irvine

Our Jim
The World's Champion

ISBN/EAN: 9783337404789

Printed in Europe, USA, Canada, Australia, Japan

Cover: Foto ©Andreas Hilbeck / pixelio.de

More available books at **www.hansebooks.com**

own Library   Price 25 Cents

PUBLISHED QUARTERLY. NO 1, SEPTEMBER, 1892. SUBSCRIPTION, $1 PER YEAR.

'OUR JIM'

(ILLUSTRATED)

The World's Champion

THE GREAT FIGHT IN DETAIL

YISH FIGHTS, LOVE EPISODES, RACY ANECDOTES—
HOW CORBETT BECAME A FIGHTER.

THE CROWN PUBLISHING CO.

ROSE ST., NEW YORK,   1203 MARKET ST., SAN FRANCISCO

Entered in the San Francisco Post Office as second class matter.

"OUR JIM"

(ILLUSTRATED)

THE WORLD'S CHAMPION

"OUR JIM."

CHAPTER I.

HEROES WIN OUR LOVE.

IN ALL AGES MEN HAVE WORSHIPED THEIR FELLOW-MEN — SOME TRAITS OF HUMANITY EVERYWHERE.

Reverence for heroes is natural. In all ages of the world respect for great men has distinguished the masses. Our old ancestors made kings of their muscular heroes and placed men of great physical powers on tripods supposed to raise them nearer to heaven.

In the legends of every race tradition tells marvelous stories of the endurance of heroes. They were often clothed with the attributes of deity, and demi-gods were as common in ancient times as idols and wooden images are to-day in darkest Africa, or among the benighted Mongolians of China.

The age of steam and electricity has its gods too, its demi-gods to whom civilized races pay the tribute of their loyal praise. Literature and the churches cannot stay that irresistible impulse which makes men take off their hats to other men who have added to the usual attributes of man a longer reach of arm, a quicker eye, a more skillful delivery, Marquis of Queensberry Rules.

And so it comes that James Corbett is now our god, tarrying on the earth under the soubriquet of "Champion Jim." The world, which is a fickle jade, had tired of John L. Sullivan. It longed for a new name, for another god. Humanity likes heroes but it does not like to believe that one man is so great that none greater can ever appear. We all like to believe that what man has done man can do, therefore Corbett's victory in playing with Sullivan as a cat tosses a mouse, teaches us to believe in the possibilities of man.

And so Corbett may one day meet his better. May he be able to "stand prosperity," and to bear himself as he has hitherto done. like a gentleman, forgetting none of the obligations to friends and wife and family. If he shall live like an honorable man the world will gladly see him wear his honors thick upon him for many years to come.

CHAPTER II.

A SAN FRANCISCO BOY.

SOME RACY ANECDOTES OF THE CHAMPION'S EARLY
YEARS—"RUSHING THE GROWLER"—A LOVE
EPISODE AND A CHAMPAGNE BATH FOR A LADY.

The hero of the day, whose greatness and fame readily outrank the glories of all the presidents from Washington down; whose name is to-day on the tongues of brave men and beautiful women to the exclusion of politics, social news. cholera news and religion, is a native of San Francisco.

Corbett was born on September 1st, 1866, at San Francisco, and he grew tall and brawny beneath Californian skies and beastly San Francisco fogs. His friends say that he lived there long enough to get plenty of wind, for the raw breezes from old ocean's gray and melancholy waste swoop down upon denizens of that bleak and forbidding city as if Providence had a special grievance against the people.

In early life young Corbett used to run away from home to buy pitchers of beer for a handsome young widow who lived near the Corbett homestead. Falling into the vernacular readily like all children, who pick up slang rapidly, Jim called this pastime "rushing the growler."

One day he remained away an unusually long time and on his return his father asked him where he had been.

"Oh," said he, "Iv'e just rushed three growlers for Mrs.———."

Jim's father always remembered the odd expression, for it was the first time he ever heard it.

When the news of victory over " the Big One" reached the new Champion's father, the incident of his boy's childhood naturally sprang to his mind.

"What news?" asked Corbett's mother of her husband.

"Well," said he, "do you remember that time that the lad said he had rushed three growlers?"

"Yes, indeed well."

"Praise God, your boy has just rushed the fourth growler to a finish in 21 rounds."

"Thank God for that! I knew he would win," said Mrs. Corbett.

Corbett's father has always been very shy of reporters. He despises their dapper, cunning ways. Once, just before the Corbett-Jackson fight, the elder Corbett got interviewed "as easy as falling off from a log."

He was in Judge Rix's Police Court chatting with Clerk Kenny. A reporter sat by Kenny engaged in writing so that the old gentleman thought he was a deputy clerk.

Feeling secure he made a neat speech, foretelling Jim's victory. He was beside himself when he saw the interview in an afternoon paper the next day, and he accused Kenny of "putting up a job on him." To square himself Kenny begged the reporter to sign a statement exonerating him from any blame and setting forth the true origin of the interview.

"By the gods, then", said Mr. Corbett, "I'll never shoot off my bazoo around your office again."

Since that episode the proud father of the world's champion has not broken the silence save in monosyllables and in a most guarded way. He believes in Jim, though, and is proud of him as may be seen by the gleam that darts from his clear eyes as he strokes his beard and listens to others discuss the boy's powers.

As a boy Jim Corbett was a handsome, chivalrous fellow of proud spirit, and quite a favorite among the girls. He had no more fights than the average boy and no more striking ventures than are usual. He was always a good angler and from earlier youth he loved the water. His memory does not go back to a time when he could not row a boat. He learned to swim in the Russian river country quite late in youth. A girl some years older than himself, a girl, too, of great beauty, once caught him and kissed him as he was passing along a crowded street. He blushed and almost cried. His companions say that he felt so cut up about it that he would not pass the street of the occurrence for months. When he grew older one day he met the girl who had kissed him, in the company of a lad who is now a handsome reporter at the New City Hall. His jealousy was at once aroused; but he did not say a word. The next week, however, he began to pass the girl's house every evening. Within a month he learned the manly art of kissing, and the elder Corbett can to-day produce the evidence that he had to pay for a pair of hinges which

Jim broke off from the girl's father's gate.

Corbett was never a *roue* but he was not a celebate or a monk in early times Once, some years ago, he and Jack ——— and two young ladies imbibed a good deal of champagne at a fashionablc saloon. That was when Jim was a mere lad, sewing a few oats. In a dare-devil spirit Jack ——— challenged Corbett to give one of the girls a champagne bath. Jim felt just good enough to do it, so, observing that she was quite *decolletec* he sponged her face gently with the bubbling "water of the champagne," that comes so dear. That was one of his earlier characteristic freaks, yet there seemed to be nothing improper or vulgar about it. He was so polite and gentle that his performance seemed like the ablution of a candidate for holy honors, in some oriental religious rite.

There are many good stories of Corbett's freaks. His wife says he

is a born humorist to-day, and that
he cannot go at anything with a long
face.   Probably his inability to take
anything seriously caused him to de-
cline to take a drubbing from John L.

CHAPTER III.

HIS BOYHOOD FIGHTS.

WHAT JIM'S FAVORITE CHUM, JAMES McENROE, SAYS OF THE CHAMPION'S EARLY YEARS—BESTED BY "SCOTCHY" McDONALD.

James McEnroe, a genial gentleman about Corbett's age, says that no fellow of Corbett's age and size ever whipped him.

'Scotchy" McDonald, the athlete and ball-player, once gave Jim a hard go, according to Mr. McEnroe, but McDonald was at that time much older than Corbett. Jim never had very many fights as a boy, but when he got into a "scrap" he was always successful. None of his playmates can remember the time when he was bested by his match in age and size.

His first idea of fighting for a business was after his amateur fight with Joe Choynski, in his father's well known stables. From that time on his life's ambition was to become a hard hitter, and his hope has since been to win the heavy-weight championship of the world.

Soon after his early Choynski fight Corbett went to Salt Lake, where he sparred. Afterwards he became instructor for the Olympic Club. Soon thereafter, in a private set-to, he "did" Dick Matthews, the Australian, Once, when no one was present save his friend McEnroe, Corbett pummeled instructor Fulda in royal style. He was able to worry Professor Walter Watson, who was greatly annoyed by Corbett's skill at ducking.

From 1885 to 1888 Jim was employed in the Nevada bank, and after that he worked for the Anglo-Nevada Insurance Company. He soon grew weary of so tame a life and devoted his time to the manly art.

"Jim always wanted to be a ball-player" said his young brother, Joe, "and you bet he was a good batter when he played."

To further his ambition Jim joined the Shamrock ball club, at that time one of the thriving institutions of that part of the city called Hayes valley.

It was about this period in life that he used to strip to the waist in his father's stable, and "put out" his playmates. One of the notable victories of early youth, which the boys recall with pleasure, was his triumph over Billy Gallagher, who is now a well known saloon man.

Though he loved out-door sports his friends, especially Mr. McEnroe, say he was not a swimmer until lately.

"We took Jim out in a yacht once," said he, "and tied a rope to his waist after which we threw him in the water, where he wiggled and plunged until we pulled him out. He was a land-lubber in those days sure."

Jim was educated at St Ignatius College, San Francisco, and at the College of the Sacred Heart.

Mr. Corbett was married to Miss Ollie Lake, an estimable young lady of Santa Cruz, in June, 1885. They have no children.

CHAPTER IV.

BOOKS AND SCHOOLING.

NOT A LOVER OF NOVELS BUT A MAN WRAPPED
  UP IN THE MARVELS OF ASTRONOMY—A
  REGULAR JEKYLL AND HYDE IN LITERA-
  TURE.

Ask nine out of ten of Corbett's
friends whether he is a reader and
they will say ''No, except of the
newspapers.''

The writer of this sketch asked his
relatives and best friends whether,
as a boy and in early manhood, he
read books of any kind, from novels
to philosophy.

"He never read any novels," said
his young brother, who looks mar-
velously like him, ''but he used to
read sensible books.

''What kind ?''

"Oh, I was only a kid then, but I know they were not novels."

"Why ?"

"Because they had heavy cloth and calf covers. They were not trashy or yellow backed."

Whether Jim pondered over the glories of Agamemnon and Ajax or whether he was studying J. D. Spencer's able editorials on democracy no one knows, but it is certain that at one period of Jim's life he was absorbed in the study of astronomy. The wonders of the heavens impressed him in early youth. People did not know this, and his dual life was a Jekyll and Hyde existence.

His sisters say that before he was ten years old he could do the work of a man, and he pondered gravely over the revelations of the family almanac. He could always "call the turn" on the moon's phases and on sunrise and sunset. That is where he first learned to be on time at the sound of the gong, and to be alert after each minute's rest.

The first thing that Jim ever explored outside of his own wig-wam was the city and county of San Francisco, including Buckley and his territory. It seemed wonderful to him, even in early youth, that the machinery of San Francisco should noiselessly move in response to one blind man's will, and it was the sight of Buckley and his power which first caused him to turn his eyes toward the starry heavens, and wonder whether a Supreme Being or Buckley caused the steady coming of day and night and the marvels of the "starry deep."

One day Jim picked up a newspaper which stated that Lord Ross had a telescope which would show in plain view twenty millions of stars and that every star was a world.

"Lord Ross is an Englishman is not he?" asked the lad, of Mrs. Corbett, his mother.

"Yes, my boy," replied she.

"Then America will beat that yet," he said.

In about a year later he read that the Lick telescope "would reveal ONE HUNDRED MILLIONS OF STARS," and that every star was a sun, giving light and heat to its planets or worlds.

It was at that time he decided to study astronomy. Though few of his friends are aware of it Jim Corbett admires nothing so much as to look into the dome of the eternal blue and marvel at the wonders there spread before his entranced vision.

Jim was educated far beyond the average "pug," and his laurels were won at St Ignatius, as before stated, and at the Sacred Heart, San Francisco.

Once or twice in his life the hero of September 7th had an opportunity to marry women of wealth, but he followed the impulses of his manly heart and gave his heart and hand to a gentle girl of tender heart and cultured features, Miss Lillie Lake of Santa Cruz.

More than any pugilist in the ring to-day Jim Corbett combines personal magnetism, handsome features, and a manner straightforward and honorable.

The first time the writer ever saw him was at the Reliance Club in Oakland, where Corbett was asked for some information for a newspaper. With much intelligence and politeness Mr. Corbett put himself out to get the data required. The impression he then made was that he was a man of strong personality, good heart and magnetism. Above all things he was cool and self possessed, though at the time surrounded by hundreds of excited men and women. In his fight with Sullivan he exhibited the same generalship and coolness.

CHAPTER V.

His Family—His Mother.

THE WORLD'S BEST MAN HAS A SWEET AND
NOBLE MOTHER, WHOM HE GREATLY RESEM-
BLES—HIS BELOVED SISTERS AND THEIR GOOD
SENSE.

It was the writer's privilege to be invited to the Corbett home on Hayes street, in San Francisco, the day after Sullivan's Waterloo.

There he met Mrs. Catherine Corbett, the immortal Jim's mother. She was suffering much pain from a broken arm, but she exhibited rare coolness and fortitude throughout the forenoon.

As may be imagined, neighbors and friends were calling, especially kind women who were extravagant in their congratulations.

"Does Jim get his generalship. as he does his features, from you?" asked the writer.

Mrs. Corbett, with rare modesty, was about to say "no" when the women assembled said in clear chorus, "yes!"

Mrs. Corbett is a handsome lady of gentle demeanor. Though the mother of eleven children she is well preserved and handsome.

"Did you think your boy would win?" she was asked.

"I thought he was very clever," she said, "but I was really afraid that that fellow would rush at him and hurt him."

Jim's sisters are all handsome and intelligent girls. They love their mother and are devoted to each other and to Jim.

"Please don't put too much in the papers about us," said one of them, but when they learned that it was a book which the visitor proposed to issue they courteously gave him pictures of their parents.

The Corbett home was the happiest spot in San Francisco, probably in the world, on September 8th, 1892.

All in all the Corbetts are not only a devoted but an interesting family.

MISS CATHERINE CORBETT.

There are twelve of them and one dead. Patrick Corbett, well known as "P. J.," is 58 years of age, a man of rare sense and good heart. He has many friends. Mrs. Catherine Corbett, his wife, is but a few years younger than he. Their children are: Frank, Harry, Esther, Jim, John, Teresa, Mamie, Katie, Joe and Tom.

P. J CORBETT.

P. J. Corbett is the proprietor of a large livery and undertaking business in San Francisco, in which he employs his son John as a book-keeper. Frank is a clerk in the Assessor's office in 'Frisco. Harry runs a poolroom in the Golden Gate City, and everybody knows Jim's line of business. The youngsters, Joe and Tom, are students at the Oakland Sacred Heart College. The four girls are unmarried and live at home. Frank, Harry and Jim are family men, but John has thus far escaped the matrimonial net. There is a strong family likeness throughout the group, but Kate, the youngest sister, is the picture of her pugilistic brother the features, of course, softened down. She is an acknowledged beauty.

In a recent copy of the *New York World*, appeared the following facts which are so apropos that they are submitted in detail

"Is your pugilistic ability an inheritance?" was asked of Jim not long ago.

"Well, hardly," laughed the big Californian; "my mother's brother, Tom McDonald, was a very clever collar-and-elbow wrestler, but that is the only member of our family who has come to public notice as a sport, and he never wrestled professionally. Oh, no, I'm the only black sheep. My brother Joe, I think, would turn out as a wonderful boxer if allowed to follow it up. The kid is at college now and is a great boy for baseball and all sports, but seems cut out for a boxer. He is naturally quick and active and has taken a liking to sparring, but my father will take care that he doesn't get too fond of it. One pugilist in the family is enough for him."

"Mr. Corbett looks like a man that could take care of himself if pushed to take his part," suggested the reporter.

"I guess he could, though I've never known him to fight," said Jim. "He's a 6-footer, weighs about 180 pounds and is very strong. Really,"

added he, in a pensive way, "I could
never thoroughly understand my
father. I always leaned to mother.
Father's a determined man, awfully
quick-tempered and harsh at times.
Mother is just the opposite—kind
affectionate, easy. At home I was
always with mother and the sisters—
rather soft of me, I dare say. When
father made up his mind to a
thing nothing can change him."

"Well, his obstinacy didn't stop you
fighting, did it?"

"Yes, indeed it did," replied Corbett, quickly. "That is, in a way.
He wa's determined to stop my fight
with Choynski before the California
Athletic Club for a $6,000 purse,
and I had to go off on the quiet and
fight for $1,000."

"Are your brothers 'sporty boys'?"
ventured the interviewer.

"Not exactly, with the exception
of Joe, who seems to be a second
Jim. Frank is a steady, quiet fellow. John's great point is his easy
good nature. He is a sort of go-as-

you-please fellow, taking things as they come. Nothing troubles him much. Harry is a sport in a way— that is, he'll bet his money and is in- terested in sporting matters gener- ally. He keeps a poolroom. None of them is what you would call a sporting man. Of course, they are all interested in my fight."

"I suppose Joe is your favorite brother and Katie your favorite sister?" was the reporter's conclu- sion.

'Oh, come now, don't you print anything like that," said Corbett, hastily, "because that would not be fair. I like them all equally. I'm inter- ested in Joe because he's just such a fellow as I was at his age, full of life and fond of sport Katie is the youngest sister and looks a great deal like me. But when it comes down they're all my brothers and sisters, and I love one just as much as I do the other." Then he said, softly: "I have only one favorite— my mother."

"Isn't a younger Mrs. Corbett a favorite?" pertly inquired a pretty, blonde-haired young woman, swinging in a hammock on the piazza, who had helped freshen Jim's memory on the ages of his brothers and sisters.

But the pugilist was looking steadily into space as if to conjure up the dear face in far-off California, and he made no reply.

CHAPTER VI.

CORBETT'S RECORD.

A MARVELOUS ROUND OF TRIUMPHS—YOUTH AND
SCIENCE ARE GREAT BUT THE "BIG ONE"
LONG A FAVORITE IN SPITE OF ALL.

Sullivan's record is many years older than Corbett's, and, as all know, it gave him a world-wide reputation. So great had Sullivan grown that the public had come to the belief that his equal would never appear.

Often Shakespeare's question arose and people wondered upon what meat doth this our Cæsar feed that he hath grown so great. To thousands the presumption that Corbett could whip Sullivan seemed a species of insanity, and for hours after the fight men were little less

than paralyzed at the news. Some
swore that the fight was sold, and
others, who a day before had vowed
that Sullivan was in the pink of condition suddenly switched and de-
clared that dissipation had killed
him.

Though 8 years younger than Sullivan, Corbett had made a good record before he whipped John L.
His genealogy is Celtic, like many
others of the world's athletic race.
His father is a native of County
Mayo, Ireland, and his mother is a
native of Dublin.

Corbett is very proud of his ances-
try and frequeutly makes mention of
the fact that he was named after an
uncle, Father James Corbett, who is
a priest in Ireland.

Corbett, when a boy, achieved a
name for himself as a good ball
player, playing left field for the
Olympic club and batting like a vet-
eran. While doing gymnasium work.
during the off months he took to
boxing, and soon became so clever

that his friends induced him to enter
the Olympic Athletic Club's tourna-
ment for the amateur heavy-weight
championship of the coast. He
easily punched his way through
this class, winning very quickly.
So impressive was his victory that
the Olympic Club opened negotia-
tions with him the same night to act
as its boxing instructor, and he signed
a contract with them a few days
after. He maintained the position
for over a year without engaging in
any outside contests until Jack
Burke, the well-known "Irish lad,"
stopped at 'Frisco on his way to
Australia. Corbett took Burke on,
it being his first professional battle.
The men boxed eight rounds in the
Mechanics' Pavilion, but as the
police would allow no referee no de-
cision other than that of the public's
could be rendered. It was generally
conceded that the Californian had
bested his man all the way.

This virtual victory at once made
him immensely popular in San Fran-

cisco, and he developed into a full-fledged professional pugilist, meeting and defeating the beast heavyweights on the Coast, the most important of these engagements being with Joe Choynski, who has since pushed his way into the front ranks of fighters. Corbett fought Choynski twice—the first time in a barn and the second time on the barge near Benicia. The first fight, as his friends will remember, was stopped by the Sheriff, and in the second Corbett won in the twenty-seventh round.

The Californian's fame had now become national, and he was offered a purse of $2,500 to go to New Orleans and box six rounds with Jake Kilrain. He took the first train, and proved to be easily the Baltimorean's master at the game, coming out without a mark. He then toured the country, his only engagement of importance being a four-round go with Dominick Mc-Caffrey in Brooklyn. He bested his

man. His last big battle of import-
ance was a sixty-one-round draw with
Peter Jackson before the California
Athletic Club, which afterward cre-
ated great discussion and not a little
bitter feeling between the men.

Jackson has all along claimed that
he was ready and willing at any time
to renew hostilities with Corbett, and
the latter in substance told the same
thing. Jackson's friends claim that
the black was far from being himself
the night of the battle, going into
the ring with but one sound leg and
in poor shape otherwise.

Besides those mentioned above,
Corbett has bested David Eiseman,
2 rounds; James Daley, 4 rounds;
Martin Costello ("Buffalo"), 3
rounds; Duncan McDonald of Butte
City, 4 rounds; Mike Brennan, 4
rounds, and William Miller of Australia, 3 rounds. He also recently
boxed all around Jim Hall in Chi-
cago. His go with Jo Lannon, so
far as points were concerned, illustrated Corbett's superior cleverness

but the go did not earn him much glory. Lannon always said he was engaged to box a friendly set-to, and was not in condition to fight.

SULLIVAN'S RECORD.

John L. Sullivan was born in Boston, October 15th, 1858. His most important victories were over John Donaldson, John Flood, Joe Goss, Paddy Ryan (in Mississippi, February, 1882) Charley Mitchell, Jim Elliott, Joe Collins, (known as Tug Wilson), Herbert Slade, Alf Greenfield and Jake Kilrain. The closest call he ever had was with Dominick McCaffrey. Charley Mitchell once knocked Sullivan squarely off his feet The performance stands alone in Sullivan's history.

CHAPTER VII.

CORBETT AT WORK.

A DAY AT THE GREAT PUGILIST'S TRAINING QUAR-
TERS JUST BEFORE THE FIGHT—PREPARATIONS
FOR FAME AND FORTUNE.

As good a way as the reader can
learn how Corbett trained for his
great victory is to read the following from Earle H. Eaton's pen. It
was written a few weeks before the
fight: Try to imagine a tall. lithe,
agile, young giant, with broad
brawny shoulders that Hercules
would have envied, with long muscle-
corded arms as quick to move, as
strong to strike a blow and well-nigh
as tireless as the piston rods of a
big engine; with shapely, powerful
legs that an athletic Apollo would
have thoroughly approved of; with a

strong, courageous, determined face, bright, intelligent eyes, and a thick, aggressive, unyielding black pompa· dour—imagine all this, I say—then place the young giant, clad only in the briefest of white tights, before a big leather football, which he is punching with a vim that makes the training quarters tremble, and you will have an idea how James J. Cor- bett looks when he is hard at work training for his battle with Sullivan.

If any one imagines that training for a ring contest is child's play, a day with Corbett at W. A. Brady's pretty summer cottage at Loch Ar- bour, near Asbury Park, would dis- abuse his mind of the idea. From 8 in the morning until 7:30 at night the California pugilist works like a Trojan, swimming, rowing, walking, playing handball punching the bag, sparring or wrestling with Jim Daly, working at the wrist machine or the pully weights, or taking a five or ten mile walk along the pleasant New

Jersey roads, with his faithful Scotch collie Ned at his heels.

Corbett does not rise with the sun, but at 7:45 every morning he takes a row for an hour on the lake near the Brady cottage. Then comes a hearty breakfast of fruit, oatmeal, soft boiled eggs, chops, potatoes and coffee, just such a breakfast as any man with a good appetite might sit down to. In fact, Corbett's diet, now that he weighs 187 pounds—one pound below the weight he desires —differs from everyday fare only by the absence of pastry.

An hour and a half after breakfast, when the process of digestion is comfortably under way, Corbett begins the day's work in earnest. He tosses his brown yachting cap aside, strips off his blue striped outing shirt and clad only in white trousers, armless undershirt and canvas shoes he improves the grip of his hands and strengthens his wrists and fore arms by work at the wrist machine. This muscle-making contrivance re-

sembles an ordinary water well windlass except that it is so small around
at one point that the hands can
easily clutch it.   From the windlass

a cord runs over a pulley at the ceiling and then down to weights weigh-

ing ten pounds. By turning the windlass with the hands the weights are
lifted to the ceiling and then allowed
slowly to descend.

It is quite a. simple matter to send
the weights up once, but the third or
fourth time the hands of a novice
become so cramped and tired that he
is quite willing to stop. Corbett's
muscular hands, however, will send
the weights ceilingward over eighty
times without a pause. Light exer-
cise at the pulley weights and toss-
ing the " medicine " ball follow. The
former strengthen the arms, shoulders and back, and the quaintly named
sphere, which weighs eight pounds,
and looks exactly likely like a big
overgrown baseball, performs much
the same service, as the Californian
and his companions play catch
with it.

After half an hour of this sort of
work Corbett's eyes brighten, for
handball time has come. He is an
expert player, and he says he enjoys
this part of his training more than

any other.   Once in the big handball court, surrounded by its high
board fence, Corbett plays against
four or five men, including his trainer, Bill Delany, and his sparring
partner, Jim Daley, and Corbett
usually defeats the whole aggrega-
tion with ease.   He is as agile as a
deer, and the ball must be a very dif-
ficult one indeed that Corbett fails
to return successfully.

After two or three games in the
court Corbett and Daly wrestle for
twenty minutes and then they enjoy
a bath in old ocean's surf, a few rods
distant.   When the big Californian
emerges from the water he is rubbed
down with alcohol, after which he
does justice to a plain but very pala-
table lunch.

For an hour and a half after this
repast Corbett lounges in the hammock.   Loch Arbour is a very se-
cluded place, but dozens of people
flock in daily from miles around to
see the young athlete, who is a college graduate and an ex bank clerk,

who uses the best of grammar and always deports himself like a gentleman, and whose motto differs only from that of the intrepid plainsman who painted "Pike's Peak or Bust!" on his wagon in the particular that it reads:

"Best Sullivan or bust!"

Corbett has hitched his pugilistic wagon to a star, for he declares that he will whip Sullivan and become the world's champion or leave the ring.

The strangers that call upon Corbett are nearly all well dressed, intelligent looking business men, and they usually approach the Californian with shyly extended hand and say: "Well, Mr. Corbett, glad to see you. Don't you know, but I've got a little money on you and I just wanted to drop in and wish you success."

Corbett always shakes the friendly hand, bows and says "Thank you." There is nothing of the blowhard about him. He remains silent many

times under very trying circumstances, but no matter what happens
he fixes both eyes on the world's
championship and keeps on sawing
wood.

The afternoon's work differs little
from that of the morning. For half
an hour Corbett works at the pulley
weights, doing his monotonous and
tiresome task without a sign of im-
patience or a spurring word from
trainer Delaney.

When the pulley weights begin to
get tired and the half hour has gone
into history, Corbett plays two or
three more games of handball and
then dons the gloves in the handball
court and spars for ten or fifteen
minutes with Jim Daly, the shifty
young boxer who fought a draw not
long ago with big Joe McAuliffe.
Daly did not become Corbett's sparring partner with suicidal intent,
consequently no hard blows are
struck, but Daly endeavors to corner
Corbett, while the latter practices
planting his favorite blows and then

getting away adroitly to avoid punishment.   His piercing eyes never
for an instant leave those of his opponent; he is as quick on his feet as
a cat, and in the matter of elusive-
ness the Irishman's proverbial flea
would weep pea green tears of envy
if pitted against the Californian.

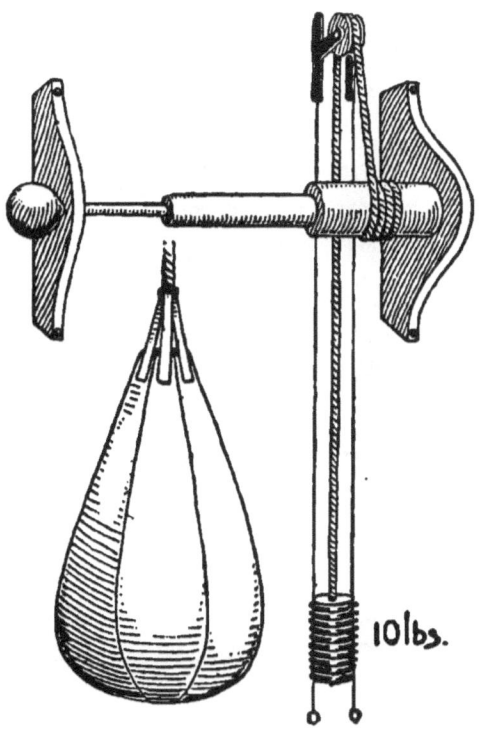

When Corbett is well warmed up by his work with Daly, he hurries into the little red barn, where the training quarters proper are located, strips himself literally to the very " buff," dons an abbreviated pair of white tights and a pair of gloves and then sails into the punching bag with a ferocity and vehemence that must make the unfortunate leather sphere heartily wish that it were once more galloping over a Lone Star State ranch on the back of a Texas steer.

For thirty minutes without a pause Corbett fights the bag as fircely as though right and left were being sent with malice prepense at the head-piece of Mr. John Lawrence Sullivan, of Boston. Again and again the bag strikes the ceiling with a re-port like a rifle shot, coming back spitefully at Corbett's head each time as it it would burst itself for joy if it could only flatten out that ag-gressive pompadour just once. Each time, however, Corbett deftly ducks his massive head; the disappointed bag misses his pompadour by a hair-breadth, and as it flies back receives a terrific short arm right hander that knocks it oblong. If Corbett wins at New Orleans that same blow will be the one that stamps the word champion on his brow.

After Corbett has punched the round bag into innocuous desuetude, he occasionally varies the monotony by making life miserable for a balloon-shaped bag of his own invention, a picture of which appears in this chapter.

The thirty minutes of bag punching is most exhaustive work, but when it is ended Corbett is as fresh as ever, and his breathing is but the merest trifle accelerated. He then gets a cold bath and a rub down, dons a sweater and is off at once for a ten-mile run and walk over rough roads. Another bath, dinner, a single good cigar, a few games of seven-up, and at 10:30 Corbett turns in for the night.

" I was never in such good condition in my life," Corbett said to the writer. " You have seen me train all day, and I want to tell you that I have worked just as faithfully every day since I have been here. I was sick when I fought Peter Jackson sixty-one rounds to a draw, but as I am in perfect condition now I expect to make the best fight of my life in September. If I win I shall defend the title of champion against all comers. If I lose I shall retire from the ring. Further than that, I only care to say that, win or lose, I shall star next season in my new play, 'Gentleman Jack.'"

The battle at the Olympic Club, New Orleans, will be for the world's championship, a purse of $25,000 and a wager of $10,000 a side, more money than was ever before fought for in the ring.

CHAPTER VIII.

JIM'S GREAT CONFIDENCE.

THE CALIFORNIA BOY SEEMED TO KNOW FROM THE
VERY OUTSET THAT HE WOULD BEST "THE BIG
ONE."

Well-based confidence marked
Corbett from the very outset. To
his friends and to reporters he often
said there was no question he would
defeat Sullivan.

More than any fighter in all history Corbett resembled Napoleon in
the unshakable confidence of his victory. He seems to have mastered
the problem of whipping Sullivan
from an intellectual point of view
long months before the fight. In
fact it was his life ambition, so when
he entered the ring the stored en-
ergies of years mounted to his brain

and nerves to give succor to his thews and sinews.

The day before the fight Jim said to a newspaper man:

"I have grown stronger and bigger, as you will see when you see me stripped. I am in a fine condition, and, though I know that Sullivan is a phenomenon, I know that I can whip him. I know that because I have seen him acting. I felt him thoroughly when we sparred at the Grand Opera House. I have studied his style of action. I know his weak points, as well as his strong, and I think I know enough to take advantage of the former and avoid the latter.

"I have been told that it is Sullivan's intention to rush me for a couple of rounds, then rest for a round and rush me again. I would like to know what sort of an opinion he has of me if he thinks he can carry out that programme. If I am so utterly at his mercy that he can do what he pleases with me in the ring,

he had better whip me in short order
and put me out of the game forever.
But after Mr. Sullivan has tried a
couple of rounds of rushing I will be
there in the ring with him, and I
have got too much sense to give him
a round of rest.   He will find that I
can keep him pretty busy, I think,
when he will want to be taking a
snooze and get ready to rush me
some more.

"There is another thing, and that
is about Mr. Sullivan's rushes.   I
understand his rushes, and I know
that it is not thrifty for any one to
let Mr. Sullivan punch them, but I
am a good bit longer in the reach
than he is, and I think I can reach
his face just a little before he can
reach my body, and neither Mr. Sullivan nor anybody else would have a
continuous appetite for rushing after
a few stiff arm-stops.   I have seen
the way Mr. Sullivan goes after a
man, beating down his guard, sending swinging blows after his ribs and
head, keeping his left to feint with

and his right to smash. The mis-
take a great many men have made
is in thinking that he meant to use
his left when he meant to use his
right. I don't mean to say that I
know more than anybody else, but it
has been in my mind to fight Sullivan for a long time. I have made a
careful study of his work. After a
time I was surprised to see how few
blows he really uses. He works on
the same order nearly all the time,
and if I am quick to evade him or
clever enough to stop him in one
round I ought to be for fifty."

"How did you get along with your
training?"

"Oh, all right. The work was
not a bit hard or distasteful, and you
can see the fix I'm in. Come around
to the Southern Club and look me
over when 1 am stripped."

"Is there anything in the fight
that you fear?" he was asked.

"I would be a fool," he said, "if I
did not know that a swinging right
from Sullivan, if it landed, might put

me out.   That is what I have got to
look out for, but the beauty of such
blows is that they cannot be de-
livered as quickly as a stab and the
fellow that is going to hit you a
knock-out blow has to telegraph you
that he is getting ready to do it.   As
far as Sullivan's infighting is concerned, I am not a bit afraid of that.
Peter Jackson was an infighter and
I had a good deal of experience with
him.

"In some respects Jackson and
Sullivan fight very much alike. They
try and keep either too far away
from you or too close to give you a
show to do them any harm.   Sullivan guards himself a little in his
rushes and then throws his weight
on you.   Jackson has very much the
same trick.   The only way to get
them when they do that is to jab
them at close quarters.   I am pretty
good at that sort of thing myself, and
you may be sure that a couple of
good stiff jabs are nearly as effective
as one full-arm blow.

"Tell the boys in San Francisco for me, and tell my friends, that I know all about the kind things they have been saying, and I appreciate them. I felt very much obliged to William Geer Harrison for the nice things he said, and to all the other boys. Tell them to paste this in their hats to-morrow night when they are in front of the bulletin board looking at the returns: If they see me get through the sixth round all right to be as confident as they please.

"Sullivan's limit for rushing is four rounds. I am going to play him for two rounds more, and if I am in the ring at the end of six rounds, the fight will be to the cleverest man with the most bottom, and I think I am that man. It is all very well for Sullivan to talk about whipping me in a punch. If he had thought he could do that I do not think he would have trained, I don't think he would have trained down from 260 pounds to 210 pounds.

I know he does not like training a
bit, and ·he did not do all the hard
work for the sake of showing his
friends that he could train. That
sort of story is a bit too gauzy to go
with me."

W. W. Naughton, who saw Corbett the day before the battle, said:

" I saw Jim Corbett this afternoon
at the Southern Athletic Club. He
was in fighting costume, just as he
will appear in the ring with Sullivan
to-morrow night. Corbett's magni-
ficent appearance surprised me, as
when he fought Jackson he was
pasty-faced and there was a lack of
muscle in his arms. Now he is
brown as a berry. His shoulder-
knobs resemble young beehives, and
his biceps and forearms are wonder-
fully developed, and his arms and
fists are the color of sole leather and
equally as hard, while around his
shoulders, back and neck there seem
to be nothing but masses of thews,
covered over with tanned and pol-
ished skin. He was a boy, so to

speak, in the Jackson fight; now he is a fully developed man."

On August 30th Jim wrote the following letter to his parents:

DEAR FOLKS—You will receive this the day before or the day of the fight, and all I can say is, keep your confidence in me. I will win in about twenty to twenty-five rounds. I am better than I ever was before and will *win* sure. Good-bye and God bless you all. Don't worry a second, I am sure to *win*.

Your loving son,

JIM."

CHAPTER IX.

RULES THAT GOVERNED THE MILL.

THE MARQUIS OF QUEENSBERRY CODE IN DETAIL, AS APPLIED TO MOST OF THE GREAT PRIZE FIGHTS.

The rules under which the great fight took place are known as the Marquis of Queensberry code, and they are very satisfactory to sporting men, being far superior in many respects to the London rules.

The following comprises the famous

MARQUIS OF QUEENSBERRY RULES.

RULE 1.—The weights of all shall be as follows: For heavy, over 158 pounds; middle, under 158 pounds and over 140 pounds; light, under

140 pounds; feather, under 120 pounds.

RULE 2.—No wrestling or hugging allowed. The rounds to be three minutes' duration, and one minute time .allowed for resting between each round.

RULE 3.—In all contests two time-keepers shall be appointed, and the referee under no circumstances shall keep time.

RULE 4.—During the contest, if either man fall through weakness or otherwise, he must get up unassisted, ten seconds being allowed him to do so; the other man meanwhile to re-tire to his corner, and when the fallen man is on his legs the round is to be resumed and continued until the three minutes have expired; and if one man fails to come to the scratch in the ten seconds allowed, the re-feree shall give his award in favor of the other man.

RULE 5.—A contestant hanging on the ropes in a helpless state, with his feet on the ground, shall be considered down. No seconds or any other persons but the referee to be allowed in the ring during the round.

RULE 6.—When either contestant is knocked down within the allotted three minutes he shall be allowed ten seconds to get on his feet again, unassisted.

RULE 7.—The gloves to be fair-sized boxing gloves of the best quality, and new. Should a glove burst or come off, it must be replaced to the referee's satisfaction. A man on his knee is considered down, and if struck while in this position it will be considered foul. No shoes or boots with spikes allowed.

RULE 8.—That any pugilist voluntarily quitting the ring previous to the deliberate judgment of the referee being obtained shall be deemed to have lost.

RULE 9.—That the seconds shall not interfere, advise or direct the adversary of their principal, and shall refrain from all offensive and irritating expressions, in all respects conducting themselves with order and decorum, and confine themselves to the diligent and careful discharge of their duties to their principals.

RULE 10.—If either man shall wilfully throw himself down without receiving a blow—whether blows shall previously have been exchanged or not—he shall be deemed to have lost the battle; but that the rule shall not apply to a man who in a close slips down from the grasp of his opponent, or from obvious accident.

RULE 11.—If a glove shall burst or come off, it must be replaced immediately to the satisfaction of the referee. Any tampering with the gloves, by forcing the hair from the gloves or otherwise, shall be considered foul.

RULE 12.—An honest and competent referee, who is familiar with the rules, shall be chosen, whose orders shall be promptly obeyed, and his decisions in all cases shall be final. In order that exhibitions may be conducted in a quiet and pleasant manner, it is suggested that the referee should always request all persons present to refrain, while a contest is in progress, from any loud expression or demonstration.

CHAPTER X.

THE GREAT FIGHT.

AN ACCQUNT OF SULLIVAN'S WATERLOO—CORBETT'S
ACCOUNT OF HOW HE BESTED THE IMMORTAL
"JOHN L."

The night of the fight, September 7th, 1892, James J. Corbett sent the following telegram to a San Francisco newspaper:

"I want all my friends to share my pleasure at success with me. I feel good, just as I expected to feel, for I have always felt sure I must win. Sullivan is big and strong, but I knew that he could not hit me. In the whole fight he never reached me with a blow.

"I have not got a scratch nor a mark on my body.

"I kept my right at reserve and cut him down with my left. When I saw I had him safe I ended it as soon as possible.

" I won by whipping him, not by keeping away.

" Please give my regards to the Olympic Club and my friends.

"JAMES J. CORBETT,
"Champion of the World."

The entrance of the gloves and Professor Duffy, the referee, at 8:45, and the first testing of the gloves by time-keeper Frank, were the first real diversions. Then there was a chance for Police Captain Barrett, who made a few brief remarks, as usual, on the necessity of silence and the peril of entering the ring before the fight was over. He found the gloves of legal size, and pronounced his benediction on the contest.

The police took their stations near the ring. The crowd held its voice for a brief space, and all craned their necks towards the corners from whence the champion and his gamy rival would come. Corbett's seconds got the lucky corner, but the chair there did not suit them. They wanted one without any back, so he could stretch out on the ropes between the rounds and get all the air possible into his chest. Ex-Mayor Guillotte picked a cork out of the ring before he made the announcement of the terms of the fight.

There was a deep scowl on Sullivan's face as he entered He looked big and burly beside his young opponent, who had a bit of a smile in his face. The difference in size about the loins was very noticeable.

Sullivan scowled some more when Captain Barrett presented Professor Duffy with a piece of silverware. He seemed to be a trifle more fleshy than he had been on Sunday, and it is likely he took on weight during the last two days. On first impression it seemed that Corbett's chance was a slim one, he looked so slight

compared with the huge man in the
other corner. He looked too good
natured, almost gentle, to be a fit
match for the scowling, determined-
looking giant in green tights.

Sullivan was lively and spoke to
his seconds in a very rough way.
His brow knitted angrily when the
referee gave the orders about break-
ing away in clinches. Trained as he
was, there was no disguising the fact
that he had more flesh than was good
for him to carry, did the fight chance
to be a long one. But he looked so
much coarser and stronger and more
brutal that one had to wonder at
Corbett's courage in facing him,
aside from his great prestige. The
spectators watched them like hounds.
not a point escaping them.

"That's a greyhound," said a
Montana sport who sat near by,
and pointed at Corbett. I felt sorry
for the lucky lad from California before the fight began. With all his
science, how could he bruise that
terrible animal in front of him? The

scowl on Sullivan's face was terrible
when the referee went to see if there
was anything under his tights,

Peopl- did not feel so sorry for Corbett when he had been in the ring
for two minutes. He skipped away
from Sullivan like a hare from a set-
ter dog. The crowd hissed and
cheered. and Sullivan's face was that
of a demon. Three minutes and not
a blow could Sullivan get in. The
Californian was too clever. I began
to feel sorry for Sullivan, and Corbett actually laughed at him and the
crowd laughed too. Was the mighty
hero to be laughed at by a slim lad?

The longer it lasted the more Corbett laughed. Then Sullivan grew
savage and rushed in. There was a
hug and Corbett's left arm slashed
across Sullivan's throat, holding him
powerless. It was a case of check-
mate, and how the house did yell.

In another rush Corbett smashed
him in the eye—smashed the champion with a left lead that made him
blind. Corbett laughed and skipped.

Sullivan was bathed in perspiration. Two straight left smashes in his august stomach from Corbett and one in the nose, made the crowd scream, and the faces of Sullivan's seconds were as black as their leader's. After the rally the Bostonian's chest heaved like a blacksmith's bellows.

Four rounds and still Corbett was not smashed through the ropes. So far from it, in fact, that Sullivan was quite respectful, and did not try any more rushes. Sullivan's friends hissed savagely when Corbett evaded. Only fancy, twelve minutes and not a blow to the credit of the champion that could have hurt a child.

Sullivan laugbed instead of scowling in the fifth. He hit savagely at long range, but his blows only hit the air. Suddenly Corbett woke up and smashed Sullivan in the face as he would hit a boy. His blows were lightning. The crowd could not see them, but they saw Sullivan's face a mass of blood, his left eye cut, his nose bleeding, and they saw a look on his face that was awful.

Again Corbett hit the big one, and his face was as Skelly's at the end of the Dixon fight. The crowd yelled themselves hoarse. Blood had whetted their appetites, and the crowd asked: " Who's the sprinter now?" It was wonderful science. Sullivan could not hit him. He knew it, and though strong and savage, had ceased to smile.

The following is Mr. Naughton's concise account of the fight by rounds:

ROUND I.

Sullivan tried a left and Corbett ducked. He caught another on his arm and hopped away from a right swing, which nearly upset Sullivan, so great was its force. Corbett danced around and the crowd began to hiss, but he only grinned and still kept away.

Sullivan made one of his famous rushes, but only found the ropes. He tried again with the same result, and his lip seemed to curl at Corbett's runaway tactics. Sullivan steadied himself a moment and tried a left at the stomach. He only found air and the crowd jeered.

Not a blow landed during the round, and as Corbett went to his corner he was cheered to the echo. He smiled in a contented fashion.

ROUND II.

Sullivan continued to feint and Jim kept hopping nimbly away. John tried a hard left hand blow and did not come within two feet of the mark. Then he tried a left at the head and missed. Sullivan then rushed and got his right home on Corbett's jaw.

There was a clinch on the ropes and Corbett's forearm went across Sullivan's throat and they separated, and as Sullivan walked to the center

of the ring Jim smashed him hard on
the mouth with his left.   John L.
made two or three lunges at the body
after that and another clumsy though
forcible   right   swing.   Corbett
dodged them.   He was still laugh-
ing and just before the gong went
off swung his left against Sullivan's
stomach.

ROUND III.

Sullivan was now looking serious.
He feinted and frowned, but Corbett
smiled and dodged. He tried a right
at the head twice and Jim was away
like a red shark.   After awhiie Corbett came back and swung his left
savagely into the champion's stomach, avoiding a return. Emboldened
by his good luck Corbett tried for
the face with both hands and got
there, while the onlookers yelled like
Comanches.
Sullivan was sweating like a bull.
He still continued to rush, one of
his blows going over the grinning
California's head.   Corbett was do-

ing famously and the Sullivanites
were looking glum.

ROUND IV.

Sullivan tried a rush and Corbett
backed away. Sullivan tried twice
more and Corbett laughingly avoided
him. Once or twice Jim dropped his
arms and gazed sarcastically at the
big fellow. More rushes from Sullivan, during which he did nothing
more serious than slap Jim once on
the back.

Corbett feinted rapidly and Sullivan's eyes widened. Then Jim
rubbed his nose playfully and skipped
away. Before the round closed he
reached Sullivan's head with a hard
right.

ROUND V.

Sullivan came from his corner with a
smile of derision. There was a left-hand
exchange on the head and Corbett put in
an extra left-hander on the face. Sullivan
got home with his left on the face and

they clinched. Then Jim worried John again with some rapid feinting, until Sullivan rushed and missed. Sullivan tried a right-hander, but Corbett smashed him on the face, bringing the blood in showers.

Now they fought savagely, Corbett doing the better work. He ducked from Sulllvan's right and peppered the champion's face with left swings until Sullivan looked gruesome. He clinched and tried to hit Corbett while hugging. Corbett broke away and punched him again and again. There was tremendous excitement.

ROUND VI.

Both men landed light lefts, and Sullivan's nose was bleeding again. The champion was beginning to look tired, for he missed his right, which was aimed for the jaw. Corbett took plenty of time and used the entire ring to maneuver in. He landed a light stomach punch and hit the champion in the face.

A little later there was a heavy exchange of lefts on the head and Sullivan seemed angry and slapped his opponent with his left hand. Corbett landed with blows on the head and ran away. The men were in the center of the ring and it began to look as though some of the fight was out of Sullivan. Corbett landed a heavy left on Sullivan's head and the champion went to his corner looking tired.

ROUND VII.

Sullivan landed on the chest with his left. Corbett responded with a left-facer. More blood trickled from the cracked bridge of Sullivan's nose. Then Corbett took the lead, getting in several nose flatteners with both hands, and also swinging his left into the body.

Sullivan's face was bathed in blood and a number said: "Out!" "He's licked!" "He's licked!" He could not counter Corbett effectively. Corbett backed him to the ropes and hit him a heavy right-hander on the damaged snout. Sullivan's back bent over the ropes and he looked anything but a world's champion. The stripling from California was playing shuttlecock and battledore with him.

ROUND VIII.

A light bodyblow from Sullivan was met by a straight left nose-disturber from

Corbett. The blood trickled again. Sullivan made a rush which was met by a right-hander which damaged his left eye. There were a couple of clinches, and some of the Sullivan men complained that Corbett forced John L.'s head back with his forearm on his throat.

Sullivan tried fighting at long range and got a brace of lefts and rights which made his puffed and bleeding face more bloody. Corbett had got down to his work and was punching his man terribly. Corbett himself did not show a scratch.

ROUND IX.

Corbett ducked under Sullivan's arm as the big fellow made a wild rush. Sullivan landed a backhander on the back of Corbett's neck. Jim steadied himself and sent a punishing left-hander on the face. Then he kept away and looked the big fellow over.

Sullivan tried to get close with his damaging left hand jab. Sullivan rushed and clinched. It looked like 2 to 1 on Corbett, and there was gloom in the Sullivan corner. Corbett smashed John L. on the wind twice with his left, then Sullivan rushed again and his lead was sent back with a stray left smash. The men were locked in each others arms when the gong sounded.

ROUND X.

The fighting now reached the point where level betting was considered a fair thing. So far the battle had all been in the Californian's favor. Sullivan put in two straights, but the force of the blows was spent before they reached Corbett's face. Sullivan got home a right-hander on the ribs and was treated to a left on his gore-covered nose. Corbett met him with the left, and by the time Sullivan had made his time-honored right swing Corbett was four feet away. Sullivan was surely tiring himself in boring tunnels through the atmosphere.

ROUND XI.

Sullivan landed a snapping left on the chest bone. He then sent in a left in the body, but received a left on the face which came in like a flash. Sullivan looked serious and fiddled for an opening. While he was working his arms Corbett got over his guard and shot a damaging left. Twice more Corbett performed the same trick, and Sullivan's face looked as if he had run against a brick wall.

Corbett put in no less than four hot punches on the stomach, and was never there when Sullivan intimated that he wished the San Franciscan to have one with him.

ROUND XII.

Corbett drove his left in on the stomach again. He did the same thing, only a good deal harder, once more, and the big fellow looked a trifle weary at the monotony of the thing. Sullivan led short a couple of times and Corbett's left countered him in good shape. He did not seem to be happy unless Sullivan's nose was red with blood. Corbett banged away on the stomach again with his left, and by way of a change put in left and right on the face. Sullivan tried another rush, but found nothing.

Corbett put in another left on the mouth and one on the stomach, and Sullivan scored a right-hander on the ribs as the round closed. It was a pretty fight, but one-sided as to the punishment.

ROUND XIII.

Neither man seemed to be blowing the least as they came to the scratch. They sparred cautiously, and Corbett did some clever dodging. Corbett seemed to be playing fast and loose,with the Bostonian.

It surely looked as if the San Franciscan neglected good openings. He contented himself during the greater part of the round with allowing Sullivan to lead, and then show him by ducking how hard it was to find a target for his blow.

ROUND XIV.

There was a good counter on the face at the start and Corbett increased his lead by swinging on the jaw with his left. Another left exchange and Corbett put two unreturned left faces to his credit. Sullivan's left eye was swollen and he began to look tired. Sullivan led for the face and got there with his left. Corbett returned the compliment in rattling style.

ROUND XV.

It looked dollars to doughnuts that Sullivan could not accomplish the knock-out he had been backed for.

Sullivan rushed, swinging savagely. He got his right home on the neck. It was a glancing blow and immediately afterwards Corbett stopped a second rush with his left and right. Sullivan's head went back with a jerk, and blood poured down his face. He sparred away for a moment, but Corbett gave him no rest. He threw his left into the stomach several times in succession. Sullivan failed to counter and Corbett still kept on pegging away at the Big Fellow's paunch.

When the round ended there was a wild scene. Those who had backed Corbett to stay longer than fifteen rounds howled with delight.

ROUND XVI.

Sullivan made a double lead and Corbett warded off both blows. Then Corbett poked his face toward his opponent in a tantalizing manner. Sullivan smashed at it, but the blow fell on James' chest. Both led with their left and scored on the face, and Corbett, as usual, threw in an extra one for good luck. The extra one started the ruby again from the bridge of Sullivan's cracked nose. Corbett went on placing left and right on the side of the head. Sullivan clinched. They stood off again and Corbett smashed him in the face hard with both hands. Odds were freely offered that Corbett would win.

ROUND XVII.

Sullivan smashed Corbett's face with his left, but the blow was only a slip. He tried again and got Corbett hard on the chin twice. Corbett stopped Sullivan's left by raising his arm.

Sullivan got in a glancing lefthander as Corbett ducked. Then Corbett sent his own left out and reached Sullivan's face solidly. Sullivan tried a rush and Corbett got away. Corbett seemed the most self-possessed mortal in the world as he went to his corner.

ROUND XVIII.

Sullivan led with his left, Corbett ducked the blow and landed one or two on Sullivan's stomach with his left before backing away. Sullivan seemed surprised. Corbett put in another left, widening the abrasion on Sullivan's swollen nose. Sullivan tried a left lead and was countered stiffly twice in succession. His lips grew bigger each moment and he seemed to grow listless in his movements.

Twice again Corbett sent his left in on the face and then Sullivan rushed. Corbett poked his left straight in the champion's face and crossed him with the right on the cheek.

Between the rounds Sullivan's seconds were busy scraping the caked sand from the soles of the champion's shoes.

ROUND XIX.

Each scored a left facer. Sullivan tried with his left for the body and missed. Corbett walked around a bit. Sullivan made a motion as if to swing his right and Corbett raised his brows and grinned. Sullivan tried to swing, but the effort was a failure. Corbett put in a couple of lefts on the stomach and then went for Sullivan's face. He smashed him twice and Sullivan went back against the ropes without trying to get even.

ROUND XX.

This was another betting round, as money had been wagered that Corbett would not last twenty rounds. He looked good for 120 as he went to the scratch and smashed Sullivan right and left in fierce style. The force of the blows sent Sullivan back and he did not regain his senses quick enough to try a counter. Corbett was on top of him again, sending in both left and right. Blood flowed from Sullivan's lips. His knees seemed to drag and he made no resistance. Then Corbett banged him right and left again, and Sullivan hung on the ropes. He was bleeding freely and seemed all but gone. The gong rang at a critical time.

ROUND XXI.

Sullivan's legs seemed to be giving out. Corbett smashed him with his left, and the blood came down the bridge of the nose again. Then Corbett went at him like a tiger. He landed out with right and left, and Sullivan's knees knocked together. He reeled to the ropes and his arms dropped.

Corbett gave him no respite. He smashed him so rapidly with both hands that the blows sounded like drum beats. Sullivan's head went from side to side, and he could not raise his hands. He began to sink to the ground slowly, Corbett keeping up the battery with both hands all the time.

Then Sullivan's eyes seemed to close and he collapsed. He fell prone on his back near the ropes, the blood gushing from nose and mouth. He was not thoroughly knocked out. He rolled over on his face, and his body, legs and green tights became covered with the damp sand. McAuliffe showered him with water from a sponge, but Sullivan was past help.

He got on his hands and fell forward on his face. Corbett stood close by ready to resume the fight should Sullivan raise, but there was no fight left in the champion. The uproar that arose was such that it drowned the sound of the gong, so Referee Duffy began to count. His voice could not be heard, but he motioned each one with his finger. He had counted ten and Sullivan was still on his face.

Delaney and Mike Donovan rushed into the ring to pull Corbett to his corner, but Jim waited to make sure that victory was his. He went close to Duffy and the latter patted him on the shoulder. That was the only signal he could give, for the booming of a thousand cannon and the roaring of a whole herd of Kansas cyclones would have been but popguns exploding to the sounds which filled the big pavilion.

CORBETT SINCE THE VICTORY.

www.ingramcontent.com/pod-product-compliance
Lightning Source LLC
Chambersburg PA
CBHW032348020726
47499CB00008B/2671